This book
belongs to:

_____

A HAWAi'i CHRiSTMAS TAiL

A HAWAI'I CHRISTMAS TAIL

WRITTEN AND ILLUSTRATED BY
RIKI INZANO

Mutual Publishing

It was time for the Humpback
Whales to make their yearly
journey across the sea for the
winter so they could enjoy a
warm Christmas in Hawai'i.
Puilani was the smallest whale
in the very last pod to leave
Alaska. Even though he was the
littlest, he had the best sense
of direction. Excited to show
off his skills and help his pod,
Puilani swam to the front to
lead the way.

ALASKA

CANADA

PACIFIC
OCEAN

HAWAII

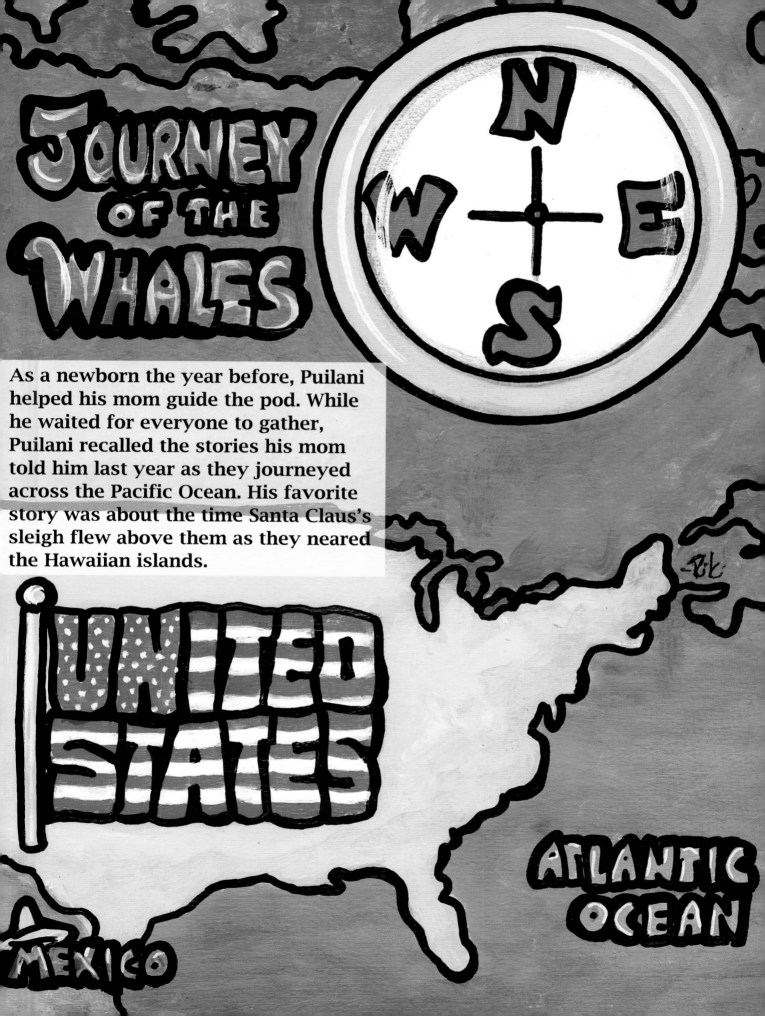

Journey of the Whales

As a newborn the year before, Puilani helped his mom guide the pod. While he waited for everyone to gather, Puilani recalled the stories his mom told him last year as they journeyed across the Pacific Ocean. His favorite story was about the time Santa Claus's sleigh flew above them as they neared the Hawaiian islands.

UNITED STATES

MEXICO

ATLANTIC OCEAN

Finally it was time to go. Puilani's mom swam close to her little son. She lightly nudged him in the right direction once or twice to keep him on course.

One evening a powerful storm interrupted their journey. Everyone swam wildly around in the swirling waves. In the confusion, Puilani was bumped so hard by another whale's tail that he tumbled away from the group in a cloud of bubbles.

When the storm calmed down and the waters stopped churning, Puilani realized he was all alone. He sang out to his pod, but there was no answer. His senses were all mixed up. He was lost.

Puilani searched deep under the sea and up close to the surface. Suddenly, he noticed a glowing red light in the snowy sky speeding towards the water. Curious, Puilani swam as quick as a flash toward the light.

Just then, the clouds parted. Puilani
clearly saw the source of the red light: It
was Santa Claus and his team of flying
reindeer! They looked just as his mom had
described them in her story.

Santa and his reindeer were headed straight for the water. With no time to lose, Puilani cleared his blowhole and sang as loud as he could to get Santa's attention.

Santa pulled on the reins with all his might. At the very last second, the sleigh changed direction and landed on Puilani's back. Santa was safe!

Santa laughed a big "Ho, Ho, Ho!" when he realized his sleigh and reindeer were on top of Puilani.

Although they were happy to be safe, the reindeer were very tired from flying through the storm. Santa scratched his head as he wondered aloud, "How are we going to deliver the last of our Christmas presents to Hawai'i?"

Puilani knew just what to do. With Santa's encouragement and guidance, Puilani set course and carried them the last few hundred miles to the Hawaiian Islands.

As they entered Hawai'i's waters the skies magically cleared. Santa pointed out a moonbow that seemed to have been put there just for them. Puilani spied his mom, just in front of his pod between Maui and Molokini. She had been looking for him. "I knew you would find your way, Puilani," she said.

Thanking the little whale, Santa and his reindeer flew off to fill the last stockings and eat the last plates of cookies. Puilani had saved Christmas for Hawai'i's keiki.

The day after Christmas, a tanned Santa paddled into the bay where Puilani was playing with his family. He had decided to stay a few weeks and give his reindeer a much needed rest.

"I want to give you a whale-sized mahalo for saving us and Christmas this year!" said Santa. He draped a huge lei around Puilani's neck. "Will you be our special guide to Hawai'i every Christmas Eve? Puilani answered yes with a big flap of his tail.

From that night on, Santa not only had his reindeer's red light to guide him, but also Puilani, the littlest whale. From his sleigh above, Santa could see Puilani's shape just below the ocean's surface, leading the way to Hawai'i.

MELEKALIKIMAKA AND A HAPPY NEW YEAR!

ABOUT THE AUTHOR

A self-taught artist and sculptor, Riki Inzano honed her skills as an apprentice and independent contractor in the film and television special effects industry in California. Inzano soon added sand sculpting to her repertoire and developed a passion for sharing this medium with kids of all ages along with her husband, Tommy, and their young son. In 2006, Inzano and her family moved to Maui to pursue their creative dreams. Her artwork has been featured in the One World Gallery and Tropical Artwear.

ISBN-10: 1-56647-932-0
ISBN-13: 978-1-56647-932-5
Library of Congress Cataloging information available upon request.

Design by Jane Gillespie
First Printing, September 2010

Mutual Publishing, LLC
1215 Center Street, Suite 210
Honolulu, Hawaii 96816
Ph: (808) 732-1709
Fax: (808) 734-4094
e-mail: info@mutualpublishing.com
www.mutualpublishing.com

Printed in China